The Think-Ups!

CLAIRE ALEXANDER

It was raining.
Anna and Kiki
were stuck inside,
wondering what
to play.

"Snakes and ladders?"
suggested Anna.
"Boring!" said Kiki.

"Hide and seek?"
asked Anna.
"But I already know
all your hiding places,"
Kiki said with a sigh.

This Walker book belongs to:

_____

_____

_____

To Mia and Molly whose love
and creativity inspired this book.
C.A.

WALKER BOOKS
AND SUBSIDIARIES
LONDON · BOSTON · SYDNEY · AUCKLAND

First published 2022 by Walker Books Ltd, 87 Vauxhall Walk, London SE11 5HJ • This edition published 2023 • © 2022 Claire Alexander
The right of Claire Alexander to be identified as author of this work has been asserted in accordance with the Copyright, Designs and Patents Act 1988 • This book has been typeset in Bodoni Egyptian Pro • Printed in China • All rights reserved.
No part of this book may be reproduced, transmitted or stored in an information retrieval system in any form or by any means, graphic, electronic or mechanical, including photocopying, taping and recording, without prior written permission from the publisher.
British Library Cataloguing in Publication Data: a catalogue record for this book is available from the British Library.
ISBN 978-1-5295-1053-9 • www.walker.co.uk • 10 9 8 7 6 5 4 3 2 1

Then Kiki had an idea.

"We could play
the Think-Ups!" she said.

"What are the Think-Ups?"
asked Anna.

"Well," said Kiki,
"all you have to do is
think up a Think-Up
and it will appear!"

"Really?" said Anna, who was not
at all sure about that.

"Watch this!" cried Kiki,
and she thought up a Think-Up.

And the Think-Up she thought up was …

a bunny!
No, not just one bunny,
but lots of bunnies!

"I'll be Kiki Flower Blossom the vet
and you can be Bob, my helper!"

"But I don't want to be Bob,
your helper," said Anna.
"I want to try a Think-Up of my own!"

So, she thought up a Think-Up,
and the Think-Up she thought up was ...

a moose!
Just one,
but a very large one!
"You may call me
Anna Wild,
the fearless explorer,"
sang Anna.

Kiki was a bit annoyed.
"OK, Bob, it's my turn now!"

And Kiki thought up another Think-Up,
and the Think-Up she thought up was ...

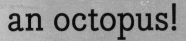
an octopus!

Not just one octopus, but lots and
lots of wriggling, giggling octopi!
"Quick, Kiki!" cried Anna. "Let's get them to the
living room!"

Anna then calmed
all the Think-Ups
down with a story.
And it was working ...

until Kiki had a secret Think-Up,
and the Think-Up she thought up was …

a koala!

Well, not just one koala, but lots and lots and lots of HUNGRY koalas!

"Oh, Kiki! What have you done?" exclaimed Anna.

"Sorry, Bob!" said Kiki.

"And please stop calling me Bob!" shouted Anna.

Then the koalas
headed for the door...

"Oh no!" cried Anna.
"They've found ...

the kitchen!"

"Kiki, your Think-Ups are TOTALLY out of control!" cried Anna.

"Well, Bob, your Moose is the biggest, messiest Think-Up ever!" shouted Kiki.

"My one moose is not as messy as all your Think-Ups!
And for the last time, my name is Anna Wild, not Bob."

"I'm sorry, Anna Wild," said Kiki.
And that's when she had an idea.
"Don't worry – I'll make it all better."

And Kiki thought up
a Think-Up, and the Think-Up
she thought up was ...

ALL

GONE!

"That was your best Think-Up yet,
Kiki Flower Blossom!"
Anna said with a smile.

Everything was back to normal,
and it had stopped raining.

"Let's go and play *you-can't-catch-me*
in the garden!" said Kiki.
"Great idea," replied Anna,
"just no more Think-Ups, OK?"

But it was already too late...

"OH, KIKI!"
shrieked Anna.

"What?" laughed Kiki. "It's only
a little can't-catch-me LION!"

CLAIRE ALEXANDER has a number of picture books to her name, including her author-illustrated books *The Think-Ups!* and the A Little Bit series. She is also the illustrator of *Puddling!*, written by Emma Perry, and *Humperdink Our Elephant Friend* and *The Snowbear*, both written by Sean Taylor. Claire teaches courses and workshops on how to write and illustrate picture books, both online and at the House of Illustration in her home city of London. Find Claire online at www.clairealexander.co.uk, on Instagram as @claire_alexander_picture_books and on Twitter as @PicBookCourse.

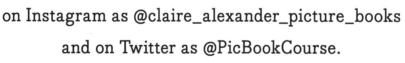

Available from all good booksellers

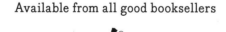

www.walker.co.uk

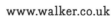